About the Author

Kevin Boon is a New Zealand author who has written plays, television programmes and over 100 books, including novels and short stories, however most of his work has been non-fiction about aspects of New Zealand history.

His most recent publication is Toby's Endeavour Voyage, which describes the amazing voyage of James Cook, his passengers and crew, aboard *H.M.S. Endeavour*, told through the eyes of an imaginary Cabin Boy, Toby Robinson.

Disillusioned by the loss of life aboard the *Endeavour*, Toby settled down to a quiet life as a country doctor, but after the death of his wife he signs on as surgeon aboard *H.M.S. Victory*, under the command of Admiral Horatio Nelson.

Kevin states, "I enjoy writing both fiction and nonfiction but I like to tell the story from the point of view of a character in the story as it enables me to describe the atmosphere and emotional situation with greater intimacy.

Toby's Victory Voyage

Kevin Boon

Toby's Victory Voyage

Olympia Publishers
London

www.olympiapublishers.com
OLYMPIA PAPERBACK EDITION

A CIP catalogue record for this title is
available from the British Library.

ISBN: 978-1-78830-423-8

This is a work of fiction.
based upon fact, but some of the characters, places and incidents
originate from the writer's imagination..

First Published in 2019

Olympia Publishers
60 Cannon Street
London
EC4N 6NP

Printed in Great Britain

I
The Call of the Sea

I never forgot the adventure I enjoyed when I sailed with Captain James Cook and his passengers and crew, as a cabin boy aboard the H.M.S. *Endeavour.* For almost three years; from 26 August 1768 to 14 July 1772 we travelled around the world, sailing through uncharted seas and visiting exotic lands.

I especially recall the four wonderful months that I spent with my Tahitian friend, Taiata, on the tropical island paradise of Tahiti. I also never forgot the six months sailing around the islands of New Zealand and the marvellous fishing and shore excursions we enjoyed. There was also the long voyage north along the east coast of Australia and the terror we all felt when we were almost shipwrecked on the Great Barrier Reef.

Those experiences lingered in my memory for a long time. Nor could I forget the tragic loss of so many of the passengers and crew, including my dear friend Taiata, as a result of the diseases they contracted when we arrived at Batavia in the Dutch East Indies. Tragically, the illnesses and deaths of the passengers and crew continued while we crossed the Indian

Ocean to South Africa. I also mourned the loss of my loyal friend and protector, Ben Johnson and the death of the irascible one-handed cook, John Thompson, with whom I worked, preparing meals for the officers and passengers during the voyage.

The deaths of so many good men convinced me that I did not want to join the navy or even go to sea again. But as someone once said, time is a great healer and circumstances change. For many years I was content with my life as a doctor in Portsmouth and my family life with my wife, daughter and son. My daughter married at a young age and went to live with her husband in London and, although I tried to discourage him, my son joined the Royal Navy as a midshipman a short time later. After my wife died, following a long battle with consumption, I found myself living alone, at the age of 45, and becoming increasingly bored with my solitary existence and career as the local doctor.

Thanks largely to my elderly uncle, a retired naval officer who had remained in close contact with many of his friends in the Admiralty, I was able to keep in touch with naval affairs. In particular I followed the later career of Captain James Cook, during his voyages to the Pacific, until his tragic death on the island of Hawaii in 1779.

I was also aware of Britain's political and military fortunes. We seemed to be almost constantly at war during my lifetime, especially with France.

After the conclusion of the Seven Years' War, which lasted from 1756 to 1763, there was a brief period of respite but hostilities were renewed when France joined the side of the American colonists when they fought for Independence in 1765. Britain's loss of the American colonies was compensated for to some extent by capturing Canada from the French. James Cook played a part in making that possible by charting the St Lawrence River, which enabled the British to capture the fortress of Quebec from the French.

The voyage of the *Endeavour* to the South Pacific also led to the expansion of the British Empire, because on the recommendations of James Cook and Joseph Banks the British Government decided to set up a penal colony at Botany Bay, on the coast of New South Wales. Gradually the colonies spread to other parts of New Holland and eventually many 'free' colonists decided to settle there of their own accord.

In France a revolution began in 1789 during which the French King and Queen were deposed and executed, along with many French noblemen and women. A 'People's Government' was formed, but eventually a brilliant military officer named Napoleon Bonaparte rose to become the French Emperor. He led France to the conquest of large areas of Europe and also into conflict with Britain.

Throughout this period the Royal Navy was Britain's greatest asset. It enabled Britain to dominate the oceans of the world, capturing huge areas of land and building a vast empire. It was often said or sung:

Rule Britannia, Britannia rules the waves,

And Britons never, never, never shall be slaves.

And:

Hearts of oak are our ships, jolly tars are our men,

We are ready; steady, boys, steady!

We'll fight and we'll conquer again and again.

Those sentiments seemed very remote from the life of a civilian doctor, who had once served as a cabin boy on His Majesty's bark *Endeavour.*

However, that situation was about to change. The first step in the process occurred when my uncle invited me to join him on a visit to the *Victory*, the great warship that had just been refurbished and virtually rebuilt in the docks at Plymouth.

I had first visited the *Victory* in 1798 when she was in a very run-down condition following the Battle of Cape St Vincent the previous year. She was being used as a hospital ship for prisoners of war at that time.

Thanks to my uncle I had acquired a reputation for treating communicable diseases and for dealing with cases of scurvy based upon my experiences on the *Endeavour*. I was commissioned by the Admiralty to visit the ship and report on the situation.

My first impression of the *Victory* was of her immense size. She was more than twice the length of the *Endeavour* and several times its tonnage. The interior space in her main decks was also impressive, although much of that space was occupied by the huge guns that were still aboard the ship. The quarters for the officers responsible for guarding the prisoners were located in the upper deck. They were well ventilated and relatively comfortable, but conditions on the two lower decks where the prisoners were held were appalling.

Fortunately there was no sign of malaria or cholera, but there were numerous other diseases present. Most of the prisoners had dysentery and many were suffering from influenza. There were also signs of scurvy due to the poor diet they were receiving.

I wrote a scathing report to the Admiralty, recommending that all the prisoners be removed from the *Victory*. The healthy prisoners should be moved to another vessel, given more time on deck and receive a diet that included fresh fruit and vegetables. The sick should be immediately moved to a healthier location, preferably on shore where they could receive appropriate medical treatment.

I realised the Admiralty would not be pleased with my report and I told my uncle that I doubted they would ever commission me for anything again. I also felt that I may have unintentionally signed a death warrant for the *Victory*. She was over thirty years old and in a very dilapidated condition. The normal life expectancy of a large warship at that time was less than twenty years. As matters eventuated, I was wrong on both counts!

The Admiralty accepted most of my recommendations and many of the prisoners were repatriated as soon as possible. Almost all of the others were given improved conditions and treatment, which enabled them to regain their health.

The *Victory* was originally going to be sent to the scrapper's yard and broken up, but she received a last-minute reprieve. It came about when one of the navy's largest vessels, the *Impregnable*, ran aground on 8 October 1799 and became a total wreck. It was decided to re-commission *Victory* as a replacement. At the beginning of 1800 she was sent to Portsmouth for extensive repairs and redevelopment.

Now, after three years' workmanship and over seventy thousand pounds spent on her, the reconstruction of the *Victory* was complete and my uncle and I had been invited to visit her.

II
A First-rate Ship of the Line

The Victory was almost unrecognisable as the same battered hulk that I visited three years previously. Once again she was a 'first-rate ship of the line', an expression used for the largest class of warships, mounting over one hundred guns. Less than a dozen such ships were launched during the eighteenth century.

She looked like a new ship, glistening with the fresh yellow and black stripes with which she had been painted. The three rows of gun-ports spaced along her sides gave her a waspish, checker-board appearance, which was later adopted by other naval vessels and called 'Nelson checker'.

She still seemed immense to me, with her overall length of 226 feet and beam of 51 feet. The three masts, or four if we count the bow-sprit, were lofty and stout and there must have been literally miles of rope involved in her rigging. It consisted of 'fixed' or 'standing' rigging, that was used to hold the masts in place against the enormous pressure that they had to withstand; and 'running' rigging that is used to raise and lower the stays and sails. The volume of timber, mostly oak, that had gone into her construction is difficult to imagine;

300,000 cubic feet by one estimate. It would have required a vast forest of more than two thousand trees to provide it.

As these thoughts were passing through my head I was suddenly brought back to the present by my uncle. "Come along, Toby, don't you want to go aboard?" he demanded impatiently.

We hurried up the sloping gangway to the quarter deck in the waste of the ship. To my surprise the captain, Thomas Hardy, and a young officer were waiting to greet us. Captain Hardy was a large and formidable-looking man, whom my uncle had met previously.

"Welcome aboard," he declared, shaking Uncle's hand. "I take it this is your nephew, Doctor Toby Robinson," he said, as he extended his hand to me. "Your uncle has told me that you were once a midshipman on James Cook's *Endeavour*," he said.

I took his hand, feeling rather embarrassed. I was never a midshipman on the *Endeavour*, just a humble cabin boy. Midshipmen are usually the sons of wealthy families, who are taken on board to train as officers. There were no midshipmen on the *Endeavour*, but I thought this was not a good time to mention that fact.

"This is Lieutenant Spearman," Captain Hardy went on. "I have asked him to show you around the ship. I have to attend a meeting, but I am hoping to see you again before you leave."

Uncle and I shook hands with the young officer as the captain strode off to his quarters at the stern of the vessel. As Lieutenant Spearman conducted us around the vessel he told us about the history of the ship.

The *Victory* had enjoyed an amazing career. She was ordered by the Admiralty in 1758; the same year that I was born, and by coincidence the same year that Admiral Horatio Nelson was born.

Her keel was laid down and her construction began at Chatham Dockyard, on 23 July 1759. After she was completed she was launched on 7 May 1764. There was some reluctance about naming her *Victory,* because the previous ship of that name had been lost with all hands in 1744.

The *Victory* did not go into action until 9 July 1778. She fought with distinction at the first Battle of Ushant. Two years later, in 1780 her hull was sheathed in copper below the waterline, in order to prevent teredo shipworm from causing damage by eating into her timbers. She fought with distinction again at the second Battle of Ushant in 1781, and in 1782 she was the flagship of Admiral Howe when he led a fleet to lift a siege on Gibraltar.

For several years the *Victory* continued to serve under a variety of captains and admirals, and fought in several minor battles without sustaining serious damage. However, her luck ran out in 1797 when she received serious damage at the Battle of Cape St. Vincent. After that she was moored as a hospital ship on the Medway, where I had visited her in 1799.

We had many questions to ask Lieutenant Spearman. Uncle began with, "How many crew will you have aboard when you sail, Lieutenant? There don't seem to be many people about at present." There were only a few 'Jack Tars' cleaning and working in the rigging.

"Oh, most of the crew haven't arrived yet," Lieutenant Spearman replied, "But we expect to have about eight hundred and twenty when we sail!"

"I remembered how amazed my uncle was, all those years ago, when he learnt that the 'little' *Endeavour* would be carrying 94 passengers and crew. This time it was my turn to be astonished. "Good Heavens! That's a huge number, even for a ship of this size!" I remarked.

It was my uncle who gave the explanation. "Well, Toby, you must understand that this is a ship of war. Some of the guns require a crew of ten or more to man them," he explained, "And there are over one hundred guns on this ship."

"One hundred and four, to be precise," Lieutenant Spearman said, "And then we have the marksmen and skirmishers required to fight on deck. If we just needed to sail the ship, we could probably manage with less than one hundred hands. Follow me, and we'll go up to the poop deck," he invited.

We ascended a flight of steps to the short deck above the stern of the ship. I remembered sufficient from my time at sea to know that the 'poop deck' had nothing to do with the latrines, which were at the bow of the ship.

"We are able to control the sails and some of the running rigging for the mizzen and main masts from here, and we also fly the signal flags when they are required," the lieutenant explained.

"I see you also have three very big signal lamps at the stern," my uncle observed.

"Yes, they are necessary for keeping in touch with other vessels in the fleet and for avoiding collisions at night," Lieutenant Spearman replied.

"Is this skylight above the captain's cabin?" I asked.

"Yes, it's above his dining cabin, but the shutters are closed at present because he is in a private meeting. The captain has three cabins on this vessel; his day and night cabins and his dining cabin." Later I was invited into the dining cabin. It was even larger than the 'great cabin' aboard the *Endeavour*. We followed the lieutenant down onto the quarter deck. It seemed a vast open space, but it had to serve many purposes. The ship's steering wheel was located at the stern, just in front of the captain's cabin. The ship's compass was set in a binnacle in front of it. In many ways it was the control centre of the ship. It was also an action-station, and there were six twelve-pounder guns along each side of the ship. I looked up at the towering masts. All three had large platforms where crow's nests were usually located.

Lieutenant Spearman explained, "We call those platforms 'tops'. As well as being observation posts they are used as battle stations for our marksmen to fire muskets at men on the decks of enemy ships. This deck is the largest open space on the ship and, as well as being used for assembling and recreation, it is also used by our sailors and marines for firing upon, and sometimes boarding, enemy ships." I tried to visualise the area crowded with men in action. It would be an extremely dangerous place and the carnage could be terrible.

"Follow me and I'll take you to the fo'c's'le," Lieutenant Spearman instructed, as he led us towards the bow of the ship. We did not go inside the fo'c's'le, which was being used by the sailors for recreational purposes, but mounted steps to the deck at the bow of the ship.

As with the other decks, it was connected to the masts by a spider-web of rigging. The huge anchors were also worked from the foredeck. There was a large ship's bell, which was used to keep time and to warn the crew in cases of emergency.

My attention was caught by two twelve-pounder guns and two massive sixty-eight-pound carronades mounted near the bow.

Lieutenant Spearman noticed me admiring them. "They are beauties, aren't they?" he remarked. "We use them when we are making a frontal attack on enemy vessels. They can do enormous damage!"

We followed the lieutenant back down the stairs to the quarter-deck and down another flight of stairs leading to the upper gun-deck, near the bow of the ship. The sickbay was located there. So were the toilets or 'heads' as they are called on ships. They were separated by partitions. Like those on the *Endeavour* they emptied directly into the ocean, but at least they were inboard, so you did not get a shower at the same time!

We made our way aft, between the rows of twelve-pounder guns, which pointed out through gun-ports on both sides of the ship. There was a wide space between them and some of the crew were using it as a work space. Near the stern we came to the admiral's quarters, which I later discovered included a huge stateroom or 'great cabin' with many windows overlooking the ship's stern.

"I'm afraid I am not permitted to take you into the admiral's quarters, even though he is not coming aboard until just before we sail. You know that Admiral Lord Nelson will be making the *Victory* his flagship when we sail?"

"Yes, I had heard that," uncle replied. "It is a great honour for the ship and for her crew," he declared.

"You never told me that, Uncle," I said indignantly. I knew my uncle followed the career of Horatio Nelson very closely.

"Well, it was supposed to be a secret," Uncle replied apologetically. He looked at Lieutenant Spearman rather accusingly.

"A secret no longer. The Admiralty announced last Thursday that Admiral Lord Horatio Nelson would be taking command of the Mediterranean Fleet, and that his flagship would be HMS *Victory*. Come, let us continue our tour," Lieutenant Spearman declared, and he led us down a flight of stairs to the middle gun-deck.

We emerged near the stern of the vessel, where the cabins and quarters of the officers were located, and we proceeded forward towards the bow of the ship. A row of fourteen twenty-four-pound guns was on either side of us. I noted that the calibre of guns increased as we descended the decks, due to their greater weight.

Near the bow was the main galley, which included a huge cast-iron 'Brodie' stove, as big as a room. It had a chimney that led up through the decks and eventually emerged at the fo'c's'le.

We descended another flight of steps to the lower gun-deck. It seemed crowded, with 15 huge thirty-two-pounder guns down both sides, and yet we were told that over 400 sailors slept there, using the regulation 14-inch hammocks slung from the ceiling. They also ate their meals on tables suspended from above. During the day everything had to be raised or stowed away.

The last deck we visited was called the 'orlop'. It contained no guns because it was below the water-line. As a result it was surprisingly roomy. It contained a large storage area for the ship's supply of food and beverages. The purser and his assistant, who were responsible for issuing them, had their cabins nearby.

I remembered the problems of supplying adequate fresh food and water for the less than one hundred people. I remarked on the challenge that it must be to supply such a great number of people on the *Victory*.

"You must remember, Toby, that you were away for almost three years on the *Endeavour*, whereas naval vessels are usually at sea for less than four months," Uncle explained.

"Yes, and there is more storage space in the hold beneath this deck, although we won't be going down there today," Lieutenant Spearman added.

There was a large area for tending to the sick or wounded in the orlop and the surgeon's cabin was nearby. However, less comforting were the huge bags of gunpowder and other combustible material that were also stored there.

"This is the safest place to store such material because it is below the waterline and the area is also protected by copper sheeting, so there is little chance of it being ignited," Lieutenant Spearman reassured us.

"Thank goodness for that! A direct hit could blow the whole ship sky-high," Uncle declared. "I notice you also store the shot and other ammunition down on this deck."

"Yes, that is because of its weight. Beneath us, in the hold we carry over 200 tons of pig-iron and shingle to act as ballast and prevent the ship from becoming top-heavy. But here I must conclude our tour because I promised the captain I would take you back to his cabin before the end of this watch." He led us up the stairs to the quarterdeck.

"Thank you for the tour, Lieutenant Spearman," my uncle said. "The *Victory* is a magnificent fighting ship."

"I will pass your compliments on to the captain," Lieutenant Spearman replied.

III
The Making of a Hero

When we arrived at the captain's day cabin, Lieutenant Spearman knocked discreetly and was called upon to enter. He returned almost immediately with good news. "The captain's meeting is over and he would like to speak to you both," he said. We followed him into the room.

"Welcome, gentlemen!" Captain Hardy said. "Did you enjoy your tour?"

"We did indeed," Uncle replied.

"Yes, I was extremely impressed with the ship," I added enthusiastically.

"That is pleasing to hear," the captain replied, "because I have a proposition to put to you, Doctor Robinson!"

"Oh, please don't call me Doctor," I said modestly. "I just like to be known as Toby, but what is this proposition, sir?" I enquired.

"Well, as you know we are in the process of signing on a crew for our next mission, and we would like you to consider taking up the position of chief surgeon and medical officer!"

For a while I was too astonished to reply. I looked at my uncle and saw that he was equally astounded. Eventually I found my tongue. "Good heavens, sir, you must be joking!" I stammered.

"I can assure you that I am not," the captain replied. "I want the best possible crew for our next voyage, no impressed men! I am aware that you came through the epic voyage of the *Endeavour* unscathed. I have also read the report that you wrote after you visited the *Victory* while she was serving as a prison ship, and the excellent advice that you provided for restoring the health of the prisoners."

"But, sir, are you aware of my age? It is over twenty years since I served aboard the *Endeavour*. I have hardly been to sea since, and I have absolutely no experience as a naval surgeon."

"You are the same age as the admiral, and he doesn't consider himself too old; and you have many years' experience of treating patients for all kinds of illnesses and injuries," the captain replied.

"But that has been in peacetime. I am not a fighting man," I said anxiously.

"I have been told by people who know you well that no one fights harder for the lives and health of their patients than Doctor Toby Robinson. You would have the rank of a warrant officer and two very experienced surgeon's mates to assist you," the captain argued.

"That is a very generous offer, sir," I replied, "but I feel I cannot accept."

After a pause the captain said, "Look, Toby, we don't sail for a few weeks. Why don't you think it over for a week or so and then let me know your answer?"

"Thank you for that, sir," I said. "I will give it a lot of thought." I left the cabin in a daze, followed by my equally dazed uncle.

I certainly had a lot of thinking to do during the week that followed Captain Hardy's proposal. At first I was certain that I would refuse his offer. However, one of the major appeals of taking up the position as chief surgeon aboard the *Victory* was the prospect of serving under the command of Admiral Horatio Nelson, whom I regarded as a heroic and fascinating figure.

My uncle had seen Nelson on several occasions, although he had never actually spoken to him. However, Uncle had studied Nelson's career and he was aware of his reputation and achievements. Others who knew him more personally described him variously as courageous, confident, inspirational, daring and even rather vain.

Horatio Nelson was born at his father's rectory at Burnham Thorp in Norfolk, on 29 September 1758. He was two months older than me. He was the sixth of the eleven children of the Reverend Edmund Nelson and his wife Catherine.

The only connection his family had with the sea or with life at sea was through Captain Maurice Suckling, one of Horatio's uncles on his mother's side of the family. That was something I had in common with him, but while my seafaring uncle tried to persuade me not to go to sea, Captain Suckling took Horatio on as a midshipman aboard the vessel he commanded, the HMS *Raisonable*, when Horatio was only twelve years old.

After a short time serving under his uncle in the navy, Horatio, like James Cook, decided to serve in the Merchant Navy: "A first-class way to develop your sea legs," he later remarked. His service with the Merchant Navy led to him making two crossings of the Atlantic Ocean, and visiting both the West and East Indies. He even travelled to the Arctic region, where it was said that he survived an encounter with a polar bear!

However, like James Cook, Horatio Nelson eventually settled on a career in the Royal Navy, and in 1776 he was appointed acting lieutenant aboard the HMS *Worcester.* The following year he became a full lieutenant on the HMS *Lowestoft.* When the American War of Independence broke out, he returned to the West Indies, where he took command of a captured tender named *Little Lucy* and he led several successful raiding expeditions.

His exploits contributed to his meteoric rise through the naval ranks and at the age of only twenty he was placed in command of the HMS *Badger.*

In 1779 Horatio Nelson was captain of HMS *Hitchinbroke.* He was sent to Nicaragua as the senior officer commanding an expedition sent to attack the fortress at San Juan.

That mission was successfully accomplished and Nelson received considerable praise and recognition for his initiative. Unfortunately, he contracted malaria in Nicaragua, and was sent back to England to recuperate.

After his recovery he was placed in command of HMS *Albemarle* and sent back to the West Indies, where he continued hunting Spanish and French merchant vessels. Even after the war was over he remained in the West Indies and commanding HMS *Boreas,* while searching for ships carrying illicit trade goods to the American colonies.

It was while in the West Indies that he met and married his wife, Frances Nesbit. A short time later they had to return to England and settled in Norfolk, while Horatio was placed on half pay, because there were few full-time positions available in the Royal Navy during peace time.

They experienced difficult times in England and it was a relief to Horatio when war with France broke out again and he was appointed captain of the sixty-four-gun vessel HMS *Agamemnon*, and he sailed to the Mediterranean with a fleet commanded by Admiral Hood.

During the successful siege of the French position Horatio received the first of several injuries that he suffered during his illustrious career. He was struck in the face by flying debris during the battle, and eventually he lost the sight of his right eye. Later this misfortune led to one of the most celebrated stories about him. At a battle near Copenhagen his commanding officer signalled that he wanted Nelson to withdraw from the battle. Nelson was reluctant to do so because he was getting the better of his opponent. He is said to have put his telescope to his blind right eye and said, "I cannot see any signal!"

It was while Horatio was in Naples that he first met Lady Emma Hamilton, who was the wife of the British Ambassador. They became very close friends for the rest of his life. It was also while he was stationed in the Mediterranean that he was promoted to captain of one of the navy's largest and most powerful vessels, HMS *Captain*.

Nelson was in command of the *Captain* when he fought against a Spanish fleet at the Battle of St Vincent in 1797. This time he was under the command of Admiral Jervis, who had the *Victory* as his flagship. Once again Nelson distinguished himself in battle.

While he was engaging the large eighty-gun Spanish galleon *St Nicholas,* a second Spanish vessel tried to come to its rescue. Nelson is said to have led his men to board the *St*

Nicholas with a cry of, "Westminster Abbey or glorious victory!" Eventually he was able to capture both of the opposing vessels.

Horatio Nelson was never afraid to expose himself to danger during the many battles he fought. On one occasion his luck ran out. In July 1797 he led a boarding party that set out in rowing boats from HMS *Theseus.* They were trying to capture the Spanish treasure ship, *Principe de Asturias*, during the battle of Santa Cruz de Tenerife. Horatio was hit in his right arm by a musket ball fired by one of the Spanish defenders. He was rowed back to the *Theseus* as quickly as possible but the ship's surgeon was unable to save his shattered right arm.

For a time, he thought his career was over, but even without his right eye and right arm he was still regarded as a brilliant commander and Britain's most popular hero. His next assignment was to lead a squadron of British ships to the Mediterranean to seek out the French fleet, which was carrying the Emperor, Napoleon Bonaparte, on a voyage of conquest.

Nelson caught up with the French off the coast of Egypt. They were at anchor in Abukir Bay, near the mouth of the River Nile. He caught them completely by surprise and, although outnumbered, he immediately went on attack. He achieved a great victory, destroying all except four of the French ships. When the news reached England, he was described as 'The Hero of the Nile'.

Recently he had been based in Britain, during a lull in the fighting against the French. Much of that time he spent with his close friend Emma Hamilton. Eventually she added a baby girl to her family. The girl was said to have been adopted, but was given the name Horatia and people drew their own conclusions. There are privileges available to national heroes.

Napoleon had not been idle during this period of peace. It was said that he was building a fleet of over three thousand ships and was planning an invasion of Britain. To avoid that, the French battle fleet would have to be destroyed and Nelson was about to go to sea to try to accomplish that task. Should I go with him? That was a question only I could answer.

I discussed the matter with my uncle who was a wonderful mentor to me, and who always had my interests at heart. At first he was appalled that I was even considering signing-on as chief surgeon aboard the *Victory*.

"You can't be serious, Toby," he responded. "Have you any idea what would be involved?"

"Yes, I believe I have," I replied. Although my voyage aboard the *Endeavour* was a long time ago, I stood up to the rigors of that long voyage. I also have had extensive experience as a medical practitioner since then, and have developed ideas about how the health of sailors at sea can be improved. I feel that the captain would not have asked me to take on that responsibility if he did not believe I could do it," I finally added.

"I know it is a great honour, Toby, and a wonderful opportunity, but you must realise there is a vast difference between this undertaking and the voyage of the *Endeavour.* That was a peaceful mission with only ninety people to care for. The *Victory* is sailing to war with over eight hundred officers, sailors and marines on board. If she goes into battle, and even if she is successful, there could be hundreds of men either killed or badly wounded, many of them dying or requiring limbs to be amputated. How would you cope with that?"

I hesitated for a while, "I honestly don't know, Uncle," I replied. "Over the years I have lost patients and I have had to amputate limbs. The captain did say that I would have two good, experienced surgeon's mates to help me, but all I can say is that I would do my best."

"I know you would, Toby, and I have always been proud of you. The final decision must be yours, but whatever you decide you will have my full support and blessing." Uncle's response surprised me and helped me make my final decision. I would report to Captain Hardy the next day - before I had a chance to change my mind!

IV
Jack and Jill Tars

I went aboard the *Victory* two weeks before she was due to sail, in order to familiarize myself with the situation where I would be living and serving as chief surgeon for the next two years. I also wanted to meet the other members of the crew with whom I would be working. The captain was there to greet me, an honour not usually provided for new crew members. He had arranged for Lieutenant Spearman, whom I had met when my uncle and I had toured the ship, to conduct me to my quarters and answer any questions that I may have. Later we became good friends.

I generally liked what I saw. My cabin in the orlop was large and, instead of the swinging hammock that I had to endure on the *Endeavour,* I had the comfort of a large cot-like bed, which was well braced against the rolling of the ship and separated from the rest of the cabin by a screen. I was also pleased with the way the rest of the cabin was laid out. It included a large desk and three chairs, an examination couch and a large array of shelves and lockers for my equipment and medical supplies. The only negative thing I noticed was the dim lighting. As the orlop was below the water-line there were no portholes or windows and it depended upon lanterns and candles for artificial lighting.

I was introduced to my associates, who were already aboard the ship and I found them much to my satisfaction. 'Coatsey' as he liked to be known, was about thirty and of rather stocky build. He had grey eyes and salt and pepper hair, cut short. He seemed rather reserved at first but very sensible and helpful.

Thomas or 'Young Tom' was a different proposition. He was full of youthful curiosity and enthusiasm. This was to be his second voyage; he had been a midshipman aboard the *Captain* on his last sailing. During that voyage he served as an assistant to the ship's surgeon and developed an interest in surgery and medical treatment. He was keen to learn everything he could from me and, although his curiosity and endless questioning could be burdensome at times, I taught him almost everything I knew.

After we got to know each other our team formed a tight unit and, along with two cabin boys who acted as stretcher bearers when needed and also helped tidy-up, we developed our own little mess group. I was also permitted to dine in the officer's wardroom and occasionally I was invited to join the captain and the senior officers in his large dining cabin. On one special occasion I had the rare privilege of dining in the admiral's superb dining suite, along with the captain and a select group of officers.

By now the ship was almost fully manned and I was staggered by the number of people (including a few women) that crowded into that huge vessel. In the whole time I was aboard I only became acquainted with relatively few of them.

After I had been aboard for a few days I made a surprising discovery. I was finishing breakfast at my desk, which our group also used as a dining table. I happened to glance across at Coatsey, who looked up and met my gaze. Suddenly it struck me: Coatsey was a woman!

Almost at the same moment she knew that I knew, and a look of anxiety clouded her face. I did not say anything because Tomas was nearby but simply mouthed the words, "It's a secret."

She nodded and gave a relieved smile, and so it remained. Coatsey later explained that she felt if it was generally known that she was a woman, it could compromise her work as a medical officer and, knowing some of the characters that we had to deal with, I suspect she was right. As far as I was concerned it made no difference to our working relationship.

Coatsey was not the only woman aboard the *Victory*. As well as those who wished to remain incognito, a few of the officers' wives were permitted to travel with them, and I met some of them while dining in the officers' wardroom.

The various other categories of personnel on the ship followed a similar pattern to that on the *Endeavour*, although of course there were no artists, scientists or other passengers. The most numerous personnel were the 'Jack Tars' or ordinary sailors who, as well as undertaking all the usual tasks involved in sailing the ship, also manned the guns when the ship went into action.

There were about a dozen ship's boys aboard, who were often given the most menial tasks, in the hope of qualifying as ordinary or 'able-bodied' seamen. Well I remembered those days, although I was relatively fortunate because there were no midshipmen on the *Endeavour*. These rather pampered individuals were actually classed as officers, although their only qualification was to be from privileged families. They were often not much older that the cabin boys and certainly no more competent, but woe betide any cabin boy who had the misfortune to serve under them. When the ship went into action the 'boys' were required to act as 'powder monkeys' carrying powder, cartridges and shot from the magazine in the orlop, to the various gun crews.

Another category of personnel that I could also recall from the *Endeavour* were the marines. On the *Endeavour* there had been only thirteen, but aboard the *Victory* there were seventy-five! Their main purpose was to fight the enemy at close quarters and occasionally board enemy vessels. As on the *Endeavour*, they saw themselves as separate and superior to the sailors, and they made little contribution to the sailing of the vessel. This feeling of superiority was heightened on the *Victory* by the fact that they were also responsible for enforcing discipline.

Gradually I met, or became familiar with, the other classes of personnel aboard the vessel. The admiral had not yet arrived but he was almost regarded as a deity, such was the fame of Lord Horatio Nelson. The prospect of serving on his flagship had made the process of recruiting a crew much easier.

The captain was the absolute ruler aboard the vessel, and the only one who could make final decisions regarding the sailing of the ship and the imposing of punishments. Captain Hardy was a benign ruler; firm but fair. He made a point of seeing me at least once a week to discuss the health of the crew and to ask if there was anything he could do to help me. Like James Cook he was an ideal person for his role.

A great deal of the practical side of sailing the ship, including navigation, sailing instructions, storage and preparation for action, was in the hands of the first lieutenant and he had several sub-lieutenants, ranked more or less in order of experience, to assist him with those tasks.

The master was responsible for the practical side of sailing the vessel, including setting and furling of sails, anchoring the ship, navigating and instructing the helmsmen. Once again he had several master's mates to assist.

There was also a group of 'warrant' or 'standing' officers, including myself, who had responsibility for various special aspects of the ship's operation. They included the surgeon, the chaplain, the ship's carpenter, the sail-maker, the chief gunnery officer, the boatswain and the purser. Of those, I felt the purser had the most influence, because he and his assistants were responsible for purchasing, storing, administering and issuing all supplies, including food and beverages. They could also sell the sailors blankets, clothes and other items. There was much scope for racketeering.

Very few of the crew had served aboard the *Victory* previously because for the last three years she had been undergoing reconstruction and prior to that she served as a hospital prison ship. However, as I mentioned previously, the captain experienced little difficulty recruiting a satisfactory crew, partly due to the reputation of the ship and its senior officers.

In particular the captain was proud of the fact that he did not need to recruit any 'impressed' men. That term referred to men who had been seized against their will, and 'pressed' into service by the 'press gangs' that operated when the navy was short of recruits.

While this activity was permitted by law, it was intended to be applied only to experienced and able-bodied sailors. However, often innocent and unsuitable individuals were seized against their wills, taken aboard ship and virtually imprisoned until the ship sailed. They rarely made good sailors and often tried to desert at the first possible opportunity.

In fact, the captain had managed to recruit an excellent crew of experienced and willing officers and sailors, who were proud of their ship and determined to serve her to the best of their abilities.

As the day for the *Victory* to sail drew nearer, the activities of settling in new crew members and supplying the vessel seemed to heighten. Finally the day came when the admiral was due to arrive and take possession of his flagship. There was an enormous sense of anticipation.

Despite the larger dimensions of the *Victory*, it was not possible to assemble the entire crew on deck, as had been the case when James Cook came aboard to take possession of the *Endeavour*. For that reason only, the officers were lined up for inspection and to greet the admiral, although all of the 75 marines were included. They appeared in clean uniforms that I had not observed them wearing previously. The rest of the crew reported to their action stations, ready for the admiral to meet them when he made a brief inspection of the ship.

It was the first time I had seen Horatio Nelson. He wore an immaculate uniform displaying all of his medals and awards. He was smaller than I expected. After the marine band played 'Rule Britannia', badly, Captain Hardy introduced the admiral to each of us as he passed along the line of officers. When my turn came, he paused and said, "I am glad you decided to sail with us, Doctor Robinson. I hope you have everything you need."

"Thank you, sir," I replied. "It is a great honour to serve under you." He gave a brief smile, before moving on down the line. He looked a little older than I had expected and appeared rather strained and tired, but he had an aura that was born of confidence and success.

After the ceremony the admiral went below deck to inspect the rest of the crew and we were dismissed to go about our normal duties. The voyage of the *Victory* was at last about to begin!

V
Life aboard the Victory

We sailed on 16 May 1803, bound for the Mediterranean. Our destination was the island of Malta, where Admiral Nelson was to take command of a fleet of British warships and blockade the French fleet in the port of Toulon. As we approached the Bay of Biscay I recalled the rough seas that I had experienced on the *Endeavour* many years ago, but on this occasion the weather and the seas were relatively calm.

Life at sea on the big warship was more complex than it was on the *Endeavour.* The crew were divided into two groups: 'Port' and 'Starboard' and they took alternate turns at being on duty in a seven-watch system. The first or 'afternoon' watch was from noon to 4 p.m. It was followed by two two-hour 'dog' watches; the first from 4 to 6 p.m. and the second from 6 to 8 p.m. There followed the 'first' watch from 8 p.m. to midnight and the 'middle' watch from midnight to 4 a.m. The 'morning' watch was from 4 to 8 a.m. and the 'forenoon' watch from 8 a.m. to mid-day. Then the whole cycle started again. The very audible ship's bell signalled the time for the watches to change.

I preferred to run my little surgery team on a more simple three-watch system, whereby Coatsey, Young Tom or myself would be on duty at the surgery for alternating eight-hour periods, in order to deal with minor accidents or illnesses, while the other two rested or enjoyed their leisure time. However, if a serious accident or problem occurred one or both of the others could be called upon.

It generally worked well, as most of the problems at this stage of the voyage were of a minor nature. I had commenced the voyage with some pre-conceived ideas about the health of sailors at sea. One of them was that the daily ration of four pints of beer and a pint of grog, which consisted of rum mixed with water in roughly equal quantities, was more than adequate. I discovered that in the past some surgeons had been inclined to supplement the grog ration with a variety of alcoholic beverages for 'medicinal' purposes. When it became known that I was not inclined to follow that practice, but tended to prescribe lime juice or some of my non-alcoholic anti-scurvy remedies, the number of unnecessary visits to the surgery tended to decline.

Contrary to popular belief, not all sailors are immune to sea-sickness: even Nelson suffered from it in his early years. Fortunately the vast majority eventually become accustomed to the motion of the sea. My treatment was a rather harsh one, but it did tend to lead to a recovery. I discovered that a mixture of rough oatmeal gruel combined with molasses tended to bring matters to a head, so to speak and gradually a more balanced diet could be substituted. On the relatively short voyage to the Mediterranean scurvy was not an issue, especially as we began with a good supply of fresh fruit and vegetables.

While on the subject of food I could not help but compare the dining arrangements for the 820 people aboard the *Victory,* with those for the 94 who had originally set sail aboard the *Endeavour.* Naturally there were major problems in terms of logistics. This was especially so when it came to the evening meals. Literally dozens of the unlucky souls, whose turn it was to arrange the cooking for their mess groups that week, had to queue for the cooked meat (usually beef, pork or fish) and the vegetables (usually rice or dried peas) prepared in the giant oven located on the middle gun deck.

I have already explained how our group formed its own mess for mealtimes. As a result, we dined better than most of the crew. I often surprised them with some of my dinner recipes developed while helping John, the one-armed cook aboard the *Endeavour.* In particular I avoided the dreaded ship's biscuits, with their liberal supply of weevils and maggots. The two ovens in the huge cooker or 'Brodie' stove were capable of baking up to eighty pounds of bread each day, and I made sure whoever was collecting the food brought back a liberal supply of fresh bread for our cabin. Along with the cheeses that I had brought aboard and any cold meat remaining from the previous evening's meal, we were able to provide our own lunches.

I have previously described the mixture of rough oatmeal gruel, combined with molasses that I used for treating sea-sickness. A similar but more watery mixture tended to be the standard 'porridge' that most sailors used for breakfast. Their name for it was 'burgoo'. I'm not sure what that meant but it seemed to fit very well. However, Coatsey found that by using a finer grain of meal and mixing it with fresh fruit when it was available, and raisons or other dried fruit when it was not, she could produce a kind of 'duff' that was very edible, especially when a drizzle of brandy was added!

We also set up a small safe in the cabin to keep left-over food as fresh as possible, and a small stove which we could use to heat it up. The meat brought down from the galley invariably consisted of pork or beef that had been boiled to rid it of salt and, occasionally, roasted. It included a large quantity of fat, bone and gristle. My most celebrated contribution was to separate out the best of the meat, lightly roast or grill it and serve it along with boiled carrots or other reasonably fresh vegetables. It was almost as popular as Coatsey's stews, which were cooked in one pot, along with a liberal supply of spices.

Generally, we ate better than many people ashore, or in the officers' mess for that matter. Meal times were also social occasions, when we were often joined by the ship's chaplain, Pastor John, and other guests. My friends seemed to never tire of me telling them about my experiences aboard the *Endeavour,* with James Cook and his passengers and crew; and especially about our visit to the South Sea Islands.

The first real test of my ability to deal with a serious accident occurred shortly after we reached Malta. It was during my rest period, while Young Tom was on duty. A serious accident occurred on deck. One of the sailors was attempting to clear a sail that had become tangled in the rigging. He lost his footing and fell to the deck. Luckily, he was not high up in the rigging and he managed to avoid landing on his head. He stretched out his arms to break his fall and had broken the lower part of one arm and badly shattered the wrist of the other.

As his comrades carried him down the stairs and into the surgery, we could hear the poor fellow screaming in agony and Young Tom became very upset. I instructed the sailors who were carrying the injured man to place him on the operating table and hold him still, and I told Tom to bring me a special brandy concoction that I used as a form of anaesthetic in such emergencies. What I would have given for some more effective form of anaesthetic, but there was none available.

I don't know whether it was shock or the effect of the brandy mixture but mercifully the young sailor passed out for a short period. Coatsey arrived and after ruefully examined the young sailor, suggested that he would probably have to lose both of his lower arms. I had other ideas. I asked her to bring me one of my wooden splints, which were curved on their inner side. After carefully straightening his broken arm I placed the splint under it and firmly bound it with a bandage at the top and bottom of the splint. I then told Coatsey to completely bind up that arm so that it could not be easily moved or jarred.

I examined the shattered wrist on the other arm more closely. It was really a mess, with many of the little bones in the wrist either broken or displaced. I knew what I had to do, and I instructed Thomas to bring me my surgical knife and saw. I cut through the flesh and sawed through the bone just below the point where the two bones of the forearm joined. There was a lot of blood, but as soon as I finished Coatsey skilfully bandaged the wound. The severed hand looked gruesome where it was and I asked Thomas, who was looking a little green at the time, to take it over to the sink. He reluctantly did so.

Finally, I instructed the crew members to move the young sailor, who was still only partially conscious, to the recovery bunk in the corner of the room and I went to wash my blood-stained hands. Lieutenant Spearman, who had been on deck duty when the accident occurred, was very impressed and complimentary about my work.

"That was absolutely marvellous, Toby," he said. "Nine surgeons out of ten would have removed both arms. You will be invaluable when we have to go into action."

"I do not like to amputate limbs if I can possibly avoid it," I replied modestly.

At that time, I had no idea of the horror, chaos and devastation that would invade the surgery when we did go into battle.

However, going into battle seemed a long way off, because when we arrived on the coast near Toulon we received news that the French fleet, under Admiral Pierre-Charles Villeneuve, had managed to evade the British blockade, and escaped into the Atlantic through the Straits of Gibraltar.

Admiral Nelson was furious when he heard that news and he immediately set out for the Atlantic to try to run them down and bring them to action.

VI
Nothing but Ocean

We made a brief visit to the harbour at Gibraltar, where Admiral Nelson was informed that the French fleet was bound for the West Indies. Few people were permitted to go ashore at Gibraltar, and only for a brief period, but Coatsey and Tom had just sufficient time to buy fresh fruit and vegetables for our mess before the *Victory* sailed.

So the chase began. The *Victory* was at the vanguard of the fleet, with the rest of the vessels spread out behind. They covered a wide area of ocean, but of course each vessel could only see as far as the horizon. It was vital to maintain communications, but that also became difficult when the weather was bad or the atmosphere misty. To my surprise I discovered the *Victory* was at least two knots faster than the *Endeavour* due to her larger area of sail. She was surprisingly manoeuvrable for a vessel of her size and bulk, although she would not have fared so well in shallow water.

The admiral was determined to catch the French fleet and bring it to action, but in such a vast area of ocean it was difficult to locate the enemy and there was a danger of missing them altogether. The wind was also often unfavourable which slowed down our progress, much to the admiral's annoyance.

In the meantime, routine life aboard the *Victory* carried on much the same as it had in the Mediterranean. When the weather permitted I liked to spend as much of my leisure time as possible on deck. On one occasion I helped to steer the ship at the helm. It took four men to control that huge wheel. On another occasion I wanted to experience the view from the platform or 'top' on the main mast. I had little difficulty scaling the rope-ladder and was enjoying the view, when the captain rather gruffly ordered me down. He reminded me that on a warship everyone should stick to their own tasks and mine were those of the chief surgeon. They did not include clambering about in the rigging.

Regarding my business as the ship's surgeon, I am pleased to say that we had no serious accidents after the young sailor, John Swift, had fallen to the deck. He was able to return to his mess after two days in the surgery, although he was forbidden to undertake activities that might place a strain on his arms. He did complain of pain in his broken arm for a time, but a moderate supply of my brandy prescription seemed to help with that.

After a few weeks we removed the binding and splint from his arm and were pleased to discover that it appeared to be healing well. There was a noticeable bump where the bone had joined, but he was able to move all of his fingers. Coatsey bound it again, without the splint, and we told him that that if he was careful with it for a few more weeks it would be as good as new.

Regarding his other arm where I had found it necessary to amputate his hand, I had a surprise in store for him. After I had cauterised the wound with a hot iron it had healed well, with a hard skin forming over the end of his forearm, just above the wrist.

In rummaging around in the cupboards of the surgery I found several hooks that were intended to be used as artificial hands, along with some wooden or 'peg' legs and other assorted items. One hook seemed well suited to my purpose. It was made from soft leather, rather like a short sleeve that could be attached to the forearm with a leather strap and buckle. At the front was a round wooden block, backed by soft padding and with a large hook, about the size of a shark hook, protruding from the front.

I called him to the surgery and asked him to try it on. I was afraid he might reject it, but instead he was delighted and fascinated by it. I never saw him without it after that. It enabled him to go about most of his normal duties. He also developed a habit of waving it about menacingly if anyone annoyed him, which earned him the nickname 'The Claw.'

A short time later a more serious accident occurred, about which I could do nothing. Once again it involved a sailor falling from the rigging, but this time it was from a greater height, and his head was the first part of his body to strike the deck. He never regained consciousness and when he arrived at the surgery he had already stopped breathing. There was nothing we could do revive him.

For the first time on the voyage death had called, and I felt as helpless and depressed as usual. Young Tom was surprised by my reaction but Coatsey sympathised and assured me that there was nothing I could have done, but the spectre of death hung over me for some time.

I discussed the matter with the chaplain, who had become a close friend during the voyage. I told him that I hated death and regarded it as an evil thing. It had robbed me of my father when I was a young boy, and then I had witnessed the death of over thirty good men, due to malaria and dysentery, during the voyage of the *Endeavour.* They included my Tahitian friend Taiata, Ben Johnson who had been my mentor and protector to me throughout the voyage and Jon Thompson, the one-armed cook with whom I had worked for many hours preparing meals for the officers and passengers. Finally, death had taken my dear wife from me shortly before the voyage.

Pastor Jon told me that I may have been confusing death with the devil or become influenced by images of him as the 'Grim Reaper' coming to steal the souls of my loved ones. But Death, he said could also be seen as an angel of mercy who relieved people of their suffering and led them on the journey to the eternal life that Jesus had promised.

I was not entirely convinced but I decided to try to forget about death and focus upon the living.

A short time after the death of the sailor who fell from the rigging, I had a surprise visitor to the surgery. There was a brief knock at the door, to which I responded with my usual invitation of 'enter.' Suddenly, standing before me was the admiral!

I stood to attention and mumbled something like, "I'm sorry, sir, I did not realise it was you."

"Oh, that's all right, Nicholson. There's no need to stand to attention. I'm sorry to have dropped in on you unexpectedly, but I just wanted a little chat."

"I am honoured by your visit, sir," I said. "Please sit down," and I motioned to my most comfortable chair. "I'm a little worried that you might be requiring my professional service."

"No, thank you. I have already lost my right eye and my right arm. I hope not to have anything else removed on this voyage," he joked.

"I am relieved to hear that, sir," I replied.

"I have been hearing about you from Captain Hardy and about what you did for the young sailor who broke both his arms in a fall to the deck. I was most impressed."

I was flattered, but modestly muttered, "I'm afraid I did not do so well with my most recent case."

"You must not be upset by that," he replied. "Death and injury are part of life on a ship at sea, especially a warship. Do you realise when we go into action there will be many seriously wounded and even dead sailors brought to you? This place will be like a charnel house. Are you prepared for that?"

I was a little taken back by that question and took some time to answer. The admiral was staring at me intently. "I have dealt with many cases over the years, but usually only one at a time. I can only say that I will do my best, and that I have two very good assistants to help me."

He seemed satisfied with my reply and, as if to change the subject, he said, "Captain Hardy has remarked upon the excellent work you have done in keeping scurvy at bay. It appears that encouraging the crew to eat fresh fruit and vegetables is part of your success. Is that something you learnt on your voyage with James Cook aboard the *Endeavour*?"

"More or less," I replied, "Although the captain himself was the main instigator, and even John, his one-handed cook, played a part."

"James Cook had a one-handed cook? Good heavens, he might have found a job for me too," he joked. "I have always been a great admirer of James Cook, but tell me how this one-handed Cook played a part in combating scurvy, it sounds like a very good story?"

I told him, "The captain had arranged for John to serve sauerkraut with a fine roast meal one evening, and he also arranged for the officers and passengers to make a great show of enjoying it. Then he had invited the wizened sail-maker, Ravenhill, who was known to be the biggest gossip on the ship, to come and see him. It was only a few days later that the captain received a request from the crew to have an allowance of sauerkraut added to their meals."

"That is a wonderful story." said the admiral, who was greatly amused. "I did not know that Cook had such imagination."

"Would you consider me impertinent if ask you whether a story about yourself is true, sir?" I asked, nervously.

"Go ahead," he replied, "although I think I can guess what it is going to be."

"Is it true that you deliberately put your telescope to your blind eye when you failed to see the signal to withdraw during the Battle of Copenhagen?" I asked.

"Well, I don't know about the 'deliberately' part. I prefer to think of it as an honest mistake," he chuckled. "But I must not keep you from your work any longer. I only wanted to tell you that we should be reaching Jamaica the day after tomorrow. If the French are still there we could be in for battle, and things would become very busy for you down here!"

He stood up, patted me on the shoulder and said, "I must have you for dinner again soon, Nicholson." With that, he departed.

VII
Preparation for Battle

The admiral was correct in his estimate that we would reach Jamaica in two days, but when we arrived he was disappointed to discover that the French had arrived a week earlier, and departed almost immediately. We may have crossed their path somewhere in the vastness of the Atlantic. He also realised that there was little chance of catching them and bringing them to action before they reached the safety of their home ports.

He was bitterly disappointed, and he felt his mission had been a failure. However, I was rather relieved and especially pleased when I realised that we would be spending a few days in Jamaica to resupply the ship, and that I would be receiving shore leave.

The tropical climate of Kingston was similar to that I had previously experienced in Tahiti and at Batavia in the Dutch East Indies. For me it did not hold the unspoiled beauty and charm of Tahiti. It was something of a melting-pot of nations and more like Batavia in character.

Fortunately, it did not have the dried-out canals of Batavia that were often used as open sewers. They were breeding grounds for malaria-carrying mosquitoes and the various forms of dysentery that caused so much devastation among the crew of the *Endeavour*. At the last officers' dinner I suggested that we should instruct the crew to be careful about what they ate and with regard to the sanitary conditions while they were ashore.

The islands of the West Indies are much larger than the relatively tiny Society Islands, such as Tahiti, but not as large as those of the East Indies. The population was very cosmopolitan, but the largest element were the people who had originally come from Africa. They had been brought to the Indies to work as slave labour on the sugar plantations, or in other forms of agricultural and manual labour. Some seemed to have gained a degree of independence but many were harshly, even cruelly treated. I was revolted by some of the things I saw, but trying to intervene would have been futile and I resolved to write about them when I returned home.

On the brighter side, there was a wonderful variety of food available. By the time we arrived, after several months at sea the food resources aboard the *Victory* were running very low. We were down to using the barrels of salted meat and fish, or 'junk' as the sailors called it. Some of them were showing early signs of scurvy by the time we arrived in Jamaica.

Available in abundance was almost every form of delicious tropical fruit that could be imagined. Fresh meat and fish were also readily available, and some of the fish was almost as delicious as those I had caught in New Zealand.

Our little mess group would be dining well for several weeks after we left the Indies. The only blot on our visit to Jamaica was that three crew members took the opportunity to abandon ship and they could not be located. They were probably men who had originally been pressed into service and had grown tired or disenchanted with life at sea. If they had been found the punishment could have been hanging at the yard-arm, but there was no sign of them before we sailed.

While there was little hope of catching up with the French and bringing them to action, the crew continued to maintain their daily exercise of reporting to action stations and practising with the ship's guns and other weapons; after all, we were a warship. My small team and I were also required to be on duty at the surgery when action stations were called, in order to prepare for the inevitable arrival of wounded personnel if we were to go into battle.

I would have liked the opportunity to observe the situation in other parts of the vessel during these exercises. In particular I was keen to witness the procedure for loading and firing the big ship's guns. I had heard their terrifying roar and felt the tremendous concussion from the huge thirty-two-pounders on the deck above us during the 'live' firing practices that took place from time to time. I was keen to see them in action.

I mentioned this to Lieutenant Spearman and he offered to ask the captain if he could arrange for me to fulfil my ambition. that opportunity came about a week later, when I was invited to observe a 'live' firing practice of a port side thirty-two-pounder on the lower gun deck, almost directly above my surgery.

While we waiting for the gunnery practice to begin, Lieutenant Spearman explained the procedure for loading and firing the guns when the ship went into action. At present the gun was in the run-out position with its muzzle protruding through its gun-port and held in position by ropes.

"When you and your uncle visited the ship, I believe I explained the various kinds of guns that we have aboard, and you are aware that they are mostly set up in rows along each side of the ship, in the three gun-decks," he began.

"Yes, if I recall correctly the guns on the upper gun-deck were fifteen twelve-pounders down each side; on the middle gun deck are fourteen twenty-four-pounders and on this gun deck, fifteen of these huge thirty-two-pound monsters. Counting the guns on the open decks, there are a total of one hundred and four guns, if I remember correctly."

"You have a remarkable memory, Toby," Lieutenant Spearman declared.

I did not mention to him that I had been counting them again recently.

I studied the huge gun that was about to go into action. The barrel, which I estimated to be about ten feet long, rested with its two metal arms or 'trunnions' in a big four-wheeled, wooden gun-carriage. At the back of the barrel was a large rounded ball of iron, which I was later told was called the 'cascable'. It had a ring at the top, through which an extremely stout rope was threaded.

"Why such a thick rope?" I questioned.

"That is called the 'breeching rope'," the lieutenant explained. "When the gun is discharged the recoil causes the carriage to run back with enormous force. Without that arresting rope it would end up on the opposite side of the ship."

"It sounds a dangerous situation. I'll make sure I'm well out of the way when the firing begins," I said ruefully.

"Did you have any guns aboard the *Endeavour*?" Lieutenant Spearman enquired.

"Only a few four-pound 'pop-guns', which were rarely used," I replied.

"Well, most of these guns **have** been fired in anger, as well as at practice and soon they will be again, if the admiral has his way," the lieutenant claimed.

"Do you think we will catch up with the French?" I asked.

"Sooner or later I believe we will, and that is why we must keep the gun crews ready for action. Did you know that our gun crews are able to maintain a rate of fire almost double that of the French?"

"No, I did not. That must be an enormous advantage," I said. "But surely not all of the guns on this side of the vessel could be fired at the same time?"

"They certainly can, it is what we call a 'broadside' and if an enemy vessel is lined up at close range, it can be completely destroyed in a single blow!"

"That is amazing. The noise must be deafening and the devastation on the enemy vessel terrible." I was awestruck.

"It is! But it is a case of destroy or be destroyed. The side that gets in the first blows usually wins. That is why we like to approach from up-wind, so that we can close the range on the enemy as quickly as possible. We also like to fire on the down-swell so that the trajectory of our shots will be into the hull of the enemy vessel, destroying their guns and their crews as quickly as possible. On the other hand, the French like to fire on the up-swells so that their fire will strike the enemy's decks, destroying masts and rigging and making the enemy vessel difficult to manoeuvre, and also killing as many of the sailors on deck as possible so that they can board the vessel."

I was silent for a while as I tried to imagine the devastation, chaos, and the dead and mangled bodies. I hoped I would never have to witness such a scene. The sound of the ships bell shocked me out of my contemplations. It was signalling the change of watch, which was also the signal for the gun-crew to assemble.

Lieutenant Spearman immediately turned over a sand-glass timer. He wanted to check how long it took the gun crew to arrive at their stations.

The first man arrived almost immediately and the next nine soon after, but the last one arrived a little late, much to the annoyance of his team-mates.

The lieutenant noted the time and muttered, "Just under three minutes. Not bad!"

From that point on the chief gun-layer gave the orders and Lieutenant Spearman simply observed. The first order was, "Run the gun in!" Immediately the crew sprang into action. One man released the gun from the restraining ring and two men hauled on ropes attached to a system of pulleys. The gun ran back to the maximum distance that the heavy restraining rope would allow, and exposing the muzzle. Another man secured the gun in position so that it could not run out again until the crew were ready to fire.

"Apply the worm!" was the next order; and one of the gunners rammed a large corkscrew-like apparatus down the muzzle and quickly withdrew it. I noted it extracted a small volume of debris, including fragments of a wooden cartridge cap and some scraps of fabric from its previous firing. The same gunner rammed a sheepskin sponge down the barrel and withdrew it again along with a small volume of dust.

"It is usually only necessary to clear the barrel after every fourth firing," Lieutenant Spearman explained, "But it is good to check that the barrel is cleared before we begin our practice. The gun is now ready for loading." He reset the glass.

The order, "Load!" was given and a bewildering set of actions followed. Each man had their task and they performed it in sequence as quickly as possible. One man had the 'cartridge', consisting of a cloth bag containing about ten pounds of gun-powder. He placed it in the mouth of the gun. The 'rammer', using a pole with a rounded wooden head that fitted closely into the barrel of the gun, rammed it home. This was followed by a wad of rope yarn, and then the 'shot', a thirty-two-pound iron ball, was sent down the barrel. It was kept in place by another wad of rope yarn. All of that was achieved with extreme speed and precision.

In the meantime the men at the opposite end of the gun had been equally busy.

As soon as the cartridge was in place the chief gunner thrust a 'priming-iron,' which was like a large needle, down the touch-hole to clear it and penetrate the cartridge. He next inserted a priming quill or fuse into the touch-hole and the gun was ready for firing.

"RUN THE GUN OUT!" was the next order and two men pulled on the ropes and tackle until the gun protruded as far as possible through the gun-port.

"FIRE!" was the final command. The chief gunner lit the fuse with a large match and—chaos!

The roar of the gun was deafening. It leapt back across the deck like a charging bull until it was finally checked by the arresting rope. Smoke and acrid fumes poured from the mouth of the gun. When they had recovered from the shock, the gun-crew gave a wild cheer.

Lieutenant Spearman checked his sand-glass timer. "Less than 90 seconds," he declared. "Run the gun back. I will be recommending you all receive an extra allowance of rum for that effort."

I remained where I stood, still stunned by the massive concussion of the gun.

"Well, Toby, what did you think of that?" Lieutenant Spearman asked.

"It was amazing," I finally stammered. "How far would the projectile be blasted?"

"Over a mile before it landed in the water," he replied. "But the range for causing maximum damage is much shorter. As short as possible," he added.

"The death and destruction that such a projectile could cause must be absolutely terrible," I mused.

"It is! Sometimes the cannon ball passes through the ship's planking and right across the deck, killing or maiming everyone in its path. The splinters from the timber blasted away also act like daggers and can cause wounding and death."

I tried to visualise the scene. "It is a terrible thing," I remarked.

"Fortunes of war," was all Lieutenant Spearman said.

VIII
A Fateful Decision

The voyage back across the Atlantic was relatively peaceful, with calm seas and no sign of the French fleet. That being the case, the admiral decide to sail directly to England, which was something of a relief for me because I had been absent from my home and family for almost two years.

I had enjoyed my time as chief surgeon and my team of assistants, including Coatsey, Young Tom and the cabin boys, were like a second family to me, while the chaplain and Lieutenant Spearman had become firm friends. We had shared many enjoyable meals together.

Our medical services were not called upon too frequently and we were able to deal with the injuries resulting from accidents reasonably successfully. Illnesses had also been relatively minor. However, it is sad to record that there were two deaths on the home voyage. One was a case of a sailor who had a serious medical condition at the beginning of the voyage and died peacefully in his sleep .

The other was the result of a mishap during a gunnery practice. One of the thirty-two-pounders broke loose from its restraining rope and a crewman was crushed between the two-ton gun and one of the deck support posts. He was still alive when he was brought to us but there was nothing we could do for him. His chest was stove in and he also had a broken hip. He died almost immediately, which was a relief because he was in terrible pain. Once again, the depressing feeling of helplessness possessed me.

When we reached Portsmouth I found my son was away at sea, but my uncle and my daughter were there to greet me. I returned to my home and resumed my life as a local medical practitioner. I was convinced my career as a naval surgeon was well and truly over.

The admiral had received a pleasant surprise when the *Victory* and the rest of the fleet arrived back in Britain. He was expecting the voyage to be regarded as a failure, because we had not brought the French fleet to action. He even believed there was the possibly of being relieved of his position as fleet commander.

However, the voyage had been reported in Britain as a 'great success' because Nelson and his fleet had prevented the French from capturing the West Indies, and had forced them to flee back to their home ports. Once again Nelson was a hero.

Three weeks after we returned to Portsmouth, I received an unexpected visitor. It was Lieutenant Spearman. I welcomed him warmly, until I realised what his mission was.

The *Victory* was due to sail again on 15 September 1805. She was to join the British fleet blockading the port of Cadiz, where the French had taken refuge and had been joined by several Spanish vessels. The lieutenant's mission was to try to persuade me to sail with them and continue my position as chief surgeon. I reminded him that I had only signed on for two years, and that my warrant had expired before the

Victory arrived back in Britain. I also told him that I had no intention of going back to sea again, but he was very persuasive.

He began by claiming that both Captain Hardy and the admiral had asked him to persuade me to sail with them again, and that they were both extremely complimentary about my ability and service as the ship's chief surgeon.

I joked about flattery, but pointed out that I had never been tested in battle and that I did not believe I could cope. Surely they could find a more experienced ship's surgeon who would do better in a battle situation.

He said they had tried, without success and that unless they found a suitable candidate for the position soon, they would have to sail without one. Coatsey and Thomas would have to share the position. He was on stronger ground there, good as they were, they often tended to disagree when I wasn't around. However, I told him that my mind was firmly made up and that any further discussion on the subject would be useless.

He reluctantly accepted the situation, and we shared a couple of glasses of brandy and some reminiscences about the voyage we had experienced .

He departed with a final reassurance that the position on the *Victory* would remain open to me.

I was utterly resolved not to change my mind, so how did it come about that I found myself walking up the gangway with my kit-bag, two weeks later? I really don't know. Could it have been loyalty to the captain and my good friends and companions aboard the **Victory**? Was it pride, or a desire to find out something about myself? It certainly wasn't naivety. I fully appreciated the enormity of the situation that I would have to face if we went into battle.

Uncle's response surprised me, as it often did. When I went to say good bye to him, he began by cautioning me. "You cannot expect to avoid going into battle as you did during your last voyage," he explained. "That was extraordinary luck. The French Admiral, Villeneuve, will realize that he cannot avoid taking on the Royal Navy under Nelson this time. He must try to destroy the British fleet if the Emperor, Napoleon Bonaparte, intends to try to invade Britain."
"Yes, I do realize that, and there is no chance of avoiding having to deal with the horror and carnage of battle this time. I can only imagine the scene of dozens of dead, dying, wounded and terribly mutilated men being brought to us in the surgery once a battle has started, but I could not live with myself if I avoided doing my duty or facing up to my worst fears; and I will not leave my young friends to try to cope with that situation without me."

It was then that Uncle showed his true feelings and loyalty, both to his country and to me. "You have made a very brave decision, Toby, for yourself, for your friends and for your country. I am proud of you. I know that you will do your best when the time comes and I will pray for you."

"Thank you, Uncle," and I embraced him.

When I arrived aboard the *Victory* the day before she sailed, on 15 September 1805 I received a warm welcome, especially from Lieutenant Spearman, Coatsey, Young Tom and Pastor John,

The first six weeks of the voyage were routine, rather like a continuation of our voyage across the Atlantic. We made our way south along the French and Spanish coasts, across the stormy Bay of Biscay to join the fleet that had been blockading the French in the port of Cadiz, under the temporary command of Vice Admiral Collingwood.

The surgery was in good order, although I noticed extra bunks had been added, and that the number of canvas body-bags was increased, in preparation for the casualties expected if, or when a battle took place.

Coatsey had added to her skills. She had honed her sewing ability while preparing many of the body-bags, and she believed she could help to close wounds and reduce bleeding by sewing up serious open wounds. I congratulated her but expressed the hope that she would not need to test her new skills. Young Tom was also more confident and anxious to test himself in battle, but I do not believe he imagined the situation that was about to unfold.

IX
The Battle of Trafalgar

By the beginning of October, the *Victory* had joined the rest of the British fleet that had taken up station outside Cadiz, where the French and Spanish ships were holed up. The admiral kept the bulk of his ships out to sea, so that he would be able to use the prevailing westerly wind to quickly close on the enemy and prevent them from running back to port. He sent four small frigates to keep watch on the harbour.

On 18 October one of the frigates, HMS *Euryalus* reported that the entire enemy fleet had left the harbour. The admiral immediately ordered his fleet to hold a position to the west, and allow the enemy to get well out to sea before we attacked. In fact, the combined French and Spanish fleet out-numbered the British by thirty-three ships-of-the-line to Nelson's twenty-seven, but that did nothing to curb Nelson's offensive spirit.

At 4 a.m. on the morning of 21 October 1805 the enemy fleet was observed, strung out in line to the east. It seemed endless. Nelson immediately turned to attack, capitalising on the favourable wind. The weather was dark and brooding, as if anticipating the coming storm. Nelson divided the fleet into two columns, the first led by Vice Admiral Collingwood in the *Royal Sovereign* and the second led by himself in the *Victory*.

Lieutenant Spearman explained that the admiral was intending to split the enemy fleet into sections, and cause confusion by separating Admiral Villeneuve and his flagship from the rest of his fleet. He added that he felt it was a bold strategy because our ships would be exposed to broadsides from the enemy, until we had cut between them and begun pouring broadsides into their vulnerable bow and stern sections. Suddenly I had to abandon my observations from the quarter-deck, as a glance from the captain indicated it was time for me to descend to my own action station in the surgery.

Everything was in good order and Coatsey, Young Tom and the others were waiting in nervous anticipation for the battle to begin. As if to confirm that battle was about to be joined, Admiral Nelson's famous message, which was sent out to all the ships in the fleet was relayed down to us in the surgery: '*England expects every man will do his duty!*'

There followed a period of almost an hour, when very little happened, while the *Victory* was closing in on the enemy. Suddenly there was an enormous volume of sound and vibrations as the French vessels began to send broadside after broadside into the bow sections of the English ships, which could only reply with the few guns on their foredecks. Wounded sailors began to be brought into the surgery, first in a trickle but gradually a flood.

My plan for operating the surgery seemed to be working. Coatsey and I dealt with the most serious cases on the main operating table, and Young Tom, assisted by the most competent of the boys, worked on the others. What I was not prepared for was the staggering number of patients that were brought to us and the horrendous nature of their wounds.

Some were already dead when they arrived and after Padre John said a prayer over them, they were placed on the bunks at the back of the room. Padre John proved a great asset to our surgical team. Not only did he pray for the dead and dying but he helped in many practical ways, comforting those who were suffering and boosting the morale of the rest of us.

For my part, I gritted my teeth with concentration and determination and just focused on each patient as they were brought before me. I tried to shut out my horror and sadness at the deaths and the ghastly wounds, and ignore the screams and groans of agony of the once proud and brave men who were brought down to us in what seemed to be a never-ending stream. I believe I did what had to be done. I focused on the next patient, and the next, and the next! There were some that were beyond help and I could do nothing but try to ease their pain, by giving them a potion and sending them to the bunks at the back of the room.

One man, who had been close to the side of the ship when a cannon ball struck, was badly wounded when a huge splinter of wood opened up a large section of his abdomen; I could even see his heart beating! There was surprisingly little blood and he remained amazingly calm.

Coatsey offered to try to stitch up his wound and I told her to give it a try. Fortunately he had been placed on his back and his vital organs were still in place. Amazingly, that man survived!

Sudden there was a change to the noise and commotion coming from the decks above. With a mighty roar our guns sprang into action, indicating that we had at last cut into the enemy line. We were now between enemy ships and we were pouring broadside after broadside into their bow and stern sections. Even some of the wounded found the energy to cheer. There was also a gradual reduction in the number of casualties arriving at the surgery for treatment after that.

Suddenly I felt a firm hand on my shoulder. It was Coatsey. "Why don't you take a rest? You have treated dozens of patients in the last hour," she said. I paused to take stock of the situation. The surgery was in a state of chaos. There must have been over fifty wounded men down there. Blood, gore and groaning sailors were everywhere. The number of dead at the back of the room had increased and all of the bunks were occupied. There were patients lying on the floor.

I had a plan for this situation, although I don't think the captain approved of it. The dead should be moved to the room in the bow section of the upper gun-deck that was usually reserved for sick sailors. However, I needed someone to take responsibility for moving the dead to what would become a temporary morgue. Padre John volunteered for that unpleasant task. He did not want to see the dead just cast overboard into the sea, as had been happening on deck. A big crewman with a bandaged head offered to help him and I ordered two stretcher-bearers to assist. For almost an hour they trooped up and down the many steps, carrying the deceased to what had now become the ship's morgue.

Next, I turned my attention to the many sailors who had received treatment but remained milling about in confusion. The very serious cases and those who required further treatment were allocated the spare bunks at the back of the room, but they quickly become filled. I told Coatsey to check

on the wounded and send the less serious cases to their own
quarters. I also instructed Tom to check on the patients whose
wounds were less serious or did not require further treatment
and ask them to report to their own sleeping quarters, or even
to go back on duty. I was surprised by the number who
volunteered for the second option: brave Jack Tars!

X
The Death of Lord Nelson

Suddenly there was a great commotion at the door. A group of officers and men arrived, bearing a stretcher. I recognised Lieutenant Spearman and the captain among them. We cleared a space and the bearers gently laid the wounded man on the operating table. I was appalled to discover it was the admiral!

Coatsey was horrified when she saw that the admiral had been badly wounded, and both Lieutenant Spearman and the captain were extremely distressed. His uniform was covered by a cloak to try to avoid the crew recognising him. It would be bad for morale if they realised that the admiral had been wounded. As soon as I removed the cover I saw how serious his condition was. He had been hit by a musket ball which had struck him in the shoulder and driven down through his abdomen. Fortunately, he had lost consciousness. Coatsey and I began by dressing his wound, which was still bleeding. We had to cut away part of his uniform to do so. I was surprised to find that he was still wearing his medals.

"The shot must have been fired by someone up on the mast of the enemy ship," Lieutenant Spearman explained.

"I was right alongside him when he fell," the captain said. "When I bent over him he said, 'They have done for me, Hardy. My backbone is shot through'."

That explained where the musket ball must have ended up. It had travelled down inside the admiral's body and lodged in his spine. Even if he survived, he would probably never walk again.

"Is there any hope for him?" the captain whispered.

I shook my head gravely and the captain began to reproach himself. "I begged him not to wear his full uniform, and not to stand out on the open deck."

"I think he felt that it was important for the crew to see him facing the same dangers that they faced," Lieutenant Spearman sympathised. "It could just as easily have been one of us."

"You don't think he was deliberately picked out, do you?" The captain asked.

"No, I don't. With all the smoke and confusion, I am convinced it was just a chance shot," the lieutenant reassured him.

"Shouldn't we move him to his own cabin?" I asked. I felt it was undignified to have the dying admiral among the wounded, and the groaning and crying of the ratings.

"No, you must not do that!" The captain was adamant. "His quarters were cleared when we went to action stations, and there is considerable damage up there. It is one of the most dangerous places on the ship."

As if that thought brought his own situation and responsibilities to his attention, he said, "You may stay here a little longer if you wish, Spearman, but I must return to my command," and with that he hurried away.

I was left with a problem. The captain had been quite clear that we should not move the admiral to his own cabin, but I still felt it was undignified for him to remain where he was, and there were still many wounded needing treatment. Suddenly the answer came to me. "We could take him to the bunk in my cabin. It is just next door and it would be more private and peaceful for him there."

"That sounds like a good idea," Lieutenant Spearman agreed and with the help of Padre John we carefully carried him through to my bunk. Lieutenant Spearman returned to his duties a short time later but others remained to check on the admiral and make sure he was comfortable. On one occasion he briefly regained consciousness and asked me in a quiet voice, "How goes the battle?"

"I believe it is going well, sir," I replied. It was all I could think of to say.

Then, as if to indicate he recognised me, he smiled and whispered, "You won't nip off a leg, will you, Doctor Toby?" and he lost consciousness once more. I choked back the tears and returned to my duties in the surgery, but I continued to check on him from time to time.

At approximately 2.30 p.m. the captain came rushing into the surgery. "How is the admiral?" He asked urgently.

"He is still alive, but only conscious for brief periods," I explained.

"I have wonderful news for him," the captain declared, and he rushed into the cabin, followed by the padre and myself. The admiral was still unconscious, but after I gently rubbed his cheeks for a few minutes his eyes flickered open.

"How goes the battle, Hardy?" he asked in a whisper that was barely audible.

"The battle is over!" the captain declared triumphantly. "Villeneuve has surrendered and ordered the rest of his captains to do so too. We have won a great victory!"

It is impossible to describe the joy that lit up the dying admiral's face. A short time later he lapsed back into unconsciousness.

"At least he'll die a happy man!" the captain commented, before returning to his duties.

Admiral Horatio Nelson died shortly before 4 p.m. on 21 October 1805. England had won a great victory but lost one of its greatest heroes. The following day Lieutenant Spearman gave me a copy of the prayer that the admiral had made before he went to his last battle. It was recorded by one of the officers who was with him in his quarters, just before the Battle of Trafalgar commenced. Apparently it went like this:

May the great God, whom I worship, grant my country
And for the benefit of Europe in general,
A great and glorious victory:
And may no misconduct, in anyone, tarnish it:
And may humanity after victory
be the predominant feature in the British fleet.

XI
Aftermath

After the death of Admiral Nelson, I made my way up to the open deck to inform the captain of the tragic news. As I climbed the steps I noticed the ship was rolling much more. The waves had mounted as the wind increased. I later realised the loss of sails and rigging had also affected the stability of the ship.

I decided to visit the sick-bay in the upper gun-deck, which was now a morgue. The bodies were stacked up like firewood at the back of the room. It seemed as if there were at least one hundred of them. They presented a gruesome sight, especially in the eerie silence that had followed the clamour of battle.

When I arrived on the quarter-deck a scene of utter devastation met my eyes. The ship had suffered tremendous damage, especially to its masts and rigging; and there was wreckage and debris strewn all over the deck. There were also bloodstains and other signs of human carnage. I realised that many of those who were obviously dead had simply been cast overboard, including the bodies of the enemy sailors that had tried to take the ship. The crew were still trying to clear the deck by throwing wreckage and debris into the rising sea.

The captain noticed me gazing about in bewilderment and came to join me.

"I suppose you've come to tell me that the admiral has passed away. I knew there was little hope for him," he sadly remarked.

"I'm afraid so, sir," I replied. "He never regained consciousness after you told him that we had been victorious."

"At least that was a good thing," the captain remarked. "But I must signal the news to Admiral Collingwood, who will take command of the fleet. Don't stay here on deck for too long; it looks like we're in for a storm," he added, as he rushed away.

A short time later Lieutenant Spearman, who was supervising the cleaning-up operation came to join me. "Bit of a shambles, isn't it?" he remarked. "I take it the admiral is dead?"

"Yes, there will be great sadness, both here and in England when that news gets out. What about our ship? There seems to be a great deal of damage to the sails and rigging, will she be able to sail?"

"I don't think so. We have lost our main spar and quite a lot of rigging. We may have to go under tow, but we are in no danger of sinking. Remember, I told you that the French like to fire on the upsurge and try to destroy the sails and rigging of enemy vessels so that they can no longer manoeuvre."

"Tell me what it was like up here on deck. We were rather busy down in the surgery, you know. I could only guess at how the battle was progressing. It seemed as if we took a pounding as we closed in on the enemy, but at last I heard our own guns roar into action."

"Yes, it took longer than expected to close on the enemy and we received many casualties among the sailors on the open decks and in the upper gun-deck, but once we cut between Villeneuve's flagship, the *Bucentaure* and the following vessel, the *Redoubtable*, we had the advantage, and we racked the enemy vessel's bow and stern with all our guns. Our superior rate of fire also gave us an advantage. In desperation the crew of the *Redoubtable* tried to board us, but they were driven back by a blast of grapeshot from our carronade."

"Is that when the admiral was hit?" I asked.

"Yes, just before we managed to drive them back," he replied.

"Do you think it was a deliberate shot that killed him?"

"No, I'm sure it wasn't. It would have been a difficult shot because it was fired from one of the tops on the enemy masthead, and there was a great deal of smoke and confusion about. I think it was just that the admiral's luck finally ran out. It was very near the end of the battle, too, because when I returned to the deck after helping you to move the admiral to your bunk, the enemy were starting to surrender," he concluded.

"It was near 2.30 p.m. when the captain came to tell us of the victory, and I estimate it was about 4 p.m. when the admiral died," I said.

At that point, one of the stays broke free from the rigging and crashed onto the deck as the ship lurched violently in the heaving sea.

"This storm is going to make it difficult to reach Gibraltar. Many of the ships will probably have to be taken under tow," Lieutenant Spearman remarked. "You'd better get back to your surgery and see to things there," he suggested. I needed no second invitation.

Thanks to Coatsey and Tom, the situation was almost under control in the surgery. After the dead had been moved to the morgue and the sailors who had recovered sufficiently returned to their stations. Only a few serious cases remained and there were even some spare bunks available.

About an hour later the captain arrived, along with Padre Jon and we went into my cabin where the admiral's body lay.

After a prayer and a few moments' silence, I asked the captain, "What am I to do with the admiral's body, sir?"

"That is one of the things I have come to speak to you about, Toby. Admiral Collingwood gave strict orders that we are to preserve his body until we get back to England, where he will be given a state funeral."

"Good heavens!" I declared. "That could be weeks away. I have no experience as a mortician, nor any idea of how to preserve a body for that length of time!"

"Admiral Collingwood's chief surgeon has recommended you preserve the body in a leaguer, or large cask of brandy. He knew of a case where that procedure was followed when a body had to be brought across the Atlantic Ocean and apparently it arrived in good condition," the captain explained.

"Did he offer to come and show us how to do it?" I asked.

"I'm afraid not," the captain replied, "And even if he did it would be difficult to make a ship-to-ship crossing in this storm. Admiral Collingwood had to abandon his own vessel, the ***Royal Sovereign,*** and transfer to the frigate *Euryalus* because of the terrible condition of his ship. I'm afraid you will have to do it, Toby. It is an unpleasant task, I know, but whatever I have asked you to do you have never let me down," he said sympathetically.

"I will help you, Toby," Padre John generously offered.

"What about the bodies of the sailors on the upper gun-deck?" I asked. "Are they to be buried at sea?"

"No, that would be too dangerous in these conditions. The fleet is sailing to Gibraltar, it should only take two days and they are to be buried there after a special service, which I am hoping you might supervise, Padre?"

"I will arrange that with the local clergy, sir," Padre John replied.

"Well, gentlemen, I must return to my duties. I will arrange for the leaguer and the brandy to be brought down to you and if there is anything else you need, just let me know." And with that he hurried away.

As soon as the leaguer and the brandy arrived the padre and I set about our melancholy task. The first decision we had to make was whether we should remove the admiral's clothes. The Padre suggested that, as he was wearing his dress uniform, we should leave him in it, medals and all! I readily agreed.

The next problem was how to fit him into the leaguer. We decided to strap his legs together in a bent position so that they would fit down into the cask. We also strapped his free arm to his side, while his shortened arm was tucked into the breast of his jacket in the familiar way.

We only half-filled the leaguer with brandy, so that it would not overflow when we placed the admiral's body into it.

With the help of Tom and Coatsey we gently lifted the admiral's body and lowered it into the leaguer. We had judged the spirit level almost perfectly, as it rose to just below his chin. I had the privilege of being the last person to gaze upon that famous face, as I poured in the remaining brandy into the leaguer and hammered down the lid. I must admit to shedding a few tears in the process.

"You should never feel ashamed of crying, Toby,' the padre said. "It is part of the sympathy and compassion you feel as a human being. It is a God-given grace and should not just be confined to women."

"Thank you, Padre, I will remember that," I replied, feeling a little better.

"At one stage I thought I saw the ghost of a smile on your face when we were filling the cask with brandy," the padre said, "Or was it just my imagination?"

"No, it was indeed a ghost, of sorts," I admitted.

"Please tell me about it?" the Padre asked with great interest.

"Well, when I sailed on the *Endeavour* as a cabin boy, many years ago, there was a sail-maker; a wizened, wrinkled character named Ravenhill. He was the oldest member of the crew and easily the worst drinker I have ever seen: ale, wine, rum, brandy, he could drink them all in great quantities, and yet he never seemed to become ill. Eventually his luck ran out while we were crossing the Indian Ocean and he was buried at sea. I could not help thinking that if he had been given the opportunity to be buried in a leaguer of brandy, he would probably have regarded it as a direct route to heaven!"

The padre was greatly amused by that story and we decided to celebrate the completion of our task by sharing a tot or two of the remaining brandy.

A short time later four burly crewmen came to collect the admiral's cask and take it to the middle gun-deck, where it was lashed to the mainmast, to keep it stable in rough seas, and placed under armed guard until we arrived in England.

The captain was wrong about the two-day voyage to Gibraltar. It took almost a week, and what a terrible week it was!

Many of the ships that fought in the great sea battle off Cape Trafalgar were badly damaged, including the English ships as well as the French and Spanish vessels, although only a few were completely destroyed. The loss of life was horrendous. Some ships lost their entire crews in the battle and in the storms that followed. On many ships the casualties numbered in the hundreds.

Several ships, including the *Victory,* were incapable of sailing independently, due to the damage to their masts, sails and rigging, and they had to be taken in tow by the less disabled vessels; in our case HMS *Neptune.*

This also included most of the captured Spanish and French vessels, which would be regarded as 'prizes of war' and provide rewards for both officers and ordinary seamen. Some captains and officers would receive sufficient money to enable them to retire and even the lower ranks would be well rewarded.

However, nature played a part in robbing the English sailors of the fruits of victory and adding to the death and destruction caused by the battle. The wind continued to blow from the west and the seas began to mount. Towing became increasingly hazardous, with tow-ropes breaking and collisions between the ships under tow and the vessels towing them. There was also an increasing danger of the surviving vessels being driven onto the costal rocks.

The storm never abated and eventually Admiral Collingwood ordered that the French and Spanish ships should be cut loose and abandoned to their fate. The victors were robbed of their spoils and almost all of the enemy vessels were wrecked. Admiral Collingwood ordered that the men on these ships should be taken aboard the British ships but many ships sank in the storm during the voyage to Gibraltar and thousands of crewmen drowned or were battered to death on the rugged shores. In fact, more lives were lost as a result of the storm than had been killed in the battle, making it the worst naval disaster in maritime history.

Eventually, on 28 October 1805, the remnants of Collingwood's battered fleet limped into Gibraltar Harbour to be welcomed as heroes A very moving service was conducted by Padre John and the local clergy for the seventy-six sailors, officers and marines from the *Victory* who were buried in the Trafalgar Cemetery. Everyone looked immaculate in their best uniforms and there were some inspiring speeches, especially about Admiral Nelson, but I could not help thinking about the carnage, destruction and death that I had witnessed.

During the next few days an amazing job was made of repairing the *Victory's* sails, masts and rigging, to a sufficient level that enabled her to sail to England independently, although there was still an enormous amount of work required to restore her completely. Rather ironically, the weather for the return voyage was relatively mild.

We arrived at Portsmouth on 5 December 1805, to a tumultuous greeting. The news of the great victory at Trafalgar and of Nelson's tragic death had preceded us.

I bad fond farewells to my friends and to the surgery team, and rushed up on deck. My son, daughter and a little grandson were there to greet me, as was my rather frail-looking uncle. After many warm embraces, I turned to uncle and said, "Uncle, that was *definitely* Toby's last voyage!"

Postscript

The body of Admiral Horatio Nelson travelled back to England in the cask of brandy in which we had embalmed him. It arrived on 5 December 1805 and was transferred to the yacht, *Chatham.* It was then taken up the Thames to Greenwich, where it lay in state for three days.

In the meantime, Captain Hardy sailed the damaged *Victory* up the Medway River to Chatham Dockyard, where she had originally been launched.

Nelson's funeral was a massive affair. At first he was transferred to a wooden coffin, coated with lead and eventually this was placed in a gilded casket. The casket was transferred to a barge that led a long procession of sixty vessels up the Thames River to Whitehall, while a vast crowd lined the banks.

I attended the funeral, along with some of the officers and crew of the *Victory* and numerous important dignitaries. It began on the morning of 9 January 1806, with a huge procession through the streets of London to St Paul's Cathedral. There were speeches and eulogies praising Nelson's heroic career and many tears among the vast crowd. Finally, the great man was laid to rest in a large black sarcophagus, located in the crypt immediately under the great dome of St. Paul's Cathedral. I could not help thinking of the many brave 'Jack Tars' who had also fought and lost their lives, only to be unceremoniously tossed overboard or buried in unmarked graves.

While the *Victory* was undergoing repairs, most of the crew enjoyed a long shore-leave, unfortunately without the spoils of war. Many of them joined the crew of HMS *Ocean*, which became Admiral Collingwood's flagship. I met with some, including Padre John and Young Tom, who had been promoted to chief surgeon, but none of them knew what had happened to Coatsey. She had just disappeared shortly after the *Victory* docked.

As for the *Victory,* she was the 'Great Survivor'. After being repaired and refitted as a second-rate ship she was placed in reserve. Eventually she saw action again when she was sent to the Baltic as the flagship of Admiral Saumarez, who was tasked with assisting Sweden to keep the Baltic Sea open for trade with Britain.

Finally, she was retired from active service and moored in Portsmouth Harbour, not far from my home, where she remains to the present day. Sometimes I made a sentimental visit to her.

What of myself? I kept true to my promise to uncle and never went to sea again. Uncle died, at the ripe old age of eighty-seven, a year after I returned.

I was happy to return to my medical practice, which had an increased number of patients, thanks to my reputation as chief surgeon on the *Victory.* In fact, there were rather too many patients, and some who called at rather awkward times. For that reason, I was a little grumpy when my bell rang shortly after dinner one evening. I answered it to discover a well-dressed young lady standing there.

Although there seemed something familiar about her, I did not recognise her at first. "Well, aren't you going to invite me in?" she asked with a smile.

It was Coatsey!

"Coatsey!" I cried in delight, and instinctively I embraced her. "Come in! Come in! It's wonderful to see you. You're looking fabulous," and I led her into my living room.

"I'm not 'Coatsey' any longer, but just plain Janice Cotter," she explained.

She went on to tell me that the reason she had left the ship so quickly was because she learnt that her elderly and frail mother was very ill. She went to London to nurse her but sadly she died a few weeks later.

'Coatsey – sorry Janice Cotter – had tried to set up a medical practice, but found few people were willing to be treated by a woman, so she had come to see how I was getting along in Portsmouth. She never left!

I invited her to stay with me and act as my assistant. She warned me that I might lose some patients if she did so.

I told her that it would not worry me in the least and that it would probably help get rid of some of the more difficult patients. In fact, after some initial hesitation, she was accepted by the majority of them. Many of the women preferred to see her after they had got over their initial surprise.

I had solved my business problem and also my loneliness problem at one and the same time. We were able to consult each other about difficult cases and share memories of events on the *Victory*. Gradually our relationship turned to a more personal one. We were married on 21 November 1806, and as fairy tales often conclude, we lived happily ever after.

The Death of Lord Nelson

www.ingramcontent.com/pod-product-compliance
Lightning Source LLC
Chambersburg PA
CBHW021341060726
47591CB00006B/2122